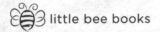 little bee books

An imprint of Bonnier Publishing USA
251 Park Avenue South, New York, NY 10010
Copyright © 2019 by Bonnier Publishing USA
All rights reserved, including the right of reproduction in whole or in part in any form. Little Bee Books is a trademark of Bonnier Publishing USA, and associated colophon is a trademark of Bonnier Publishing USA.

Library of Congress Cataloging-in-Publication Data is available upon request.

Manufactured in China   TPL 1118
ISBN 978-1-4998-0831-5 (PBK)
First Edition 10 9 8 7 6 5 4 3 2 1
ISBN 978-1-4998-0832-2 (HC)
First Edition 10 9 8 7 6 5 4 3 2 1
littlebeebooks.com
bonnierpublishingusa.com

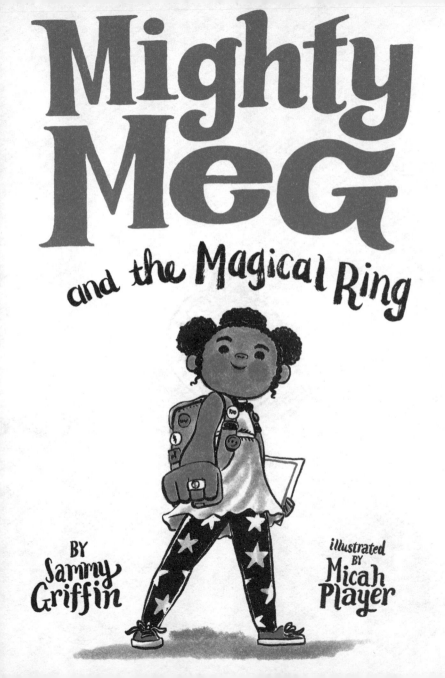

Mighty Meg
and the Magical Ring

BY
Sammy Griffin

illustrated
BY
Micah Player

Contents

Chapter One:
Meg's Perfectly Perfect Birthday Party

Meg's birthday was the most exciting thing to happen to her since her family went to Disneyland last summer. Turning eight was a big deal—like parades and fireworks big.

Her favorite people were there: Mom, her little brother Curtis, and her best friends Tara and Ruby. The only ones missing were Aunt Nikki and Uncle Derrick, but they would call Meg later.

Orange balloons hung from the lights in the living room. Orange-and-red streamers looped down from the ceiling above a stack of presents on the coffee table. A three-layer cake waited in the kitchen; Meg had already peeked at the peach frosting covered in purple sprinkles. She didn't have to check the freezer to know there was rainbow sherbet inside. Her party was practically perfect.

3

Curtis bounced on the couch, looking more excited than Meg. But that's just how her brother acted *all* the time—like his pants were on fire.

"How much longer?" he whined.

Tara and Ruby laughed while Mom came up behind him and put her calming hands on his shoulders, settling him into the cushions. "Be patient, C. It'll just be a few more minutes."

Like Curtis, Meg couldn't understand what was taking so long. Mom kept checking her watch like they were waiting on a pizza delivery or something. But they had already eaten dinner, cleared the table, and washed the dishes.

Being eight meant that Meg was more mature than Curtis and wouldn't pester Mom over and over again about when they would open presents, no matter how much she wanted to. Still, Meg watched the clock as she pulled Tara and Ruby onto the oversized recliner with her. The girls erupted in laughter as they became a tangle of arms and legs squished together.

When the doorbell rang, Mom pretended to look shocked and said a little too loudly, "I wonder who *that* is!"

Goosebumps spread on Meg's arms, and she sprang from the chair to follow Mom to the front door. Meg could tell something was going on, and she wanted to be right there when it happened.

Mom opened the door with a flair, and even though Meg had become a mature eight-year-old that day, she squealed in delight.

"Aunt Nikki!" she yelled as she barreled into her aunt's arms.

Meg's party had just become perfectly perfect!

Chapter Two:
Aunt Nikki's Adventure

Meg hadn't expected Aunt Nikki to come to her party because she had been on a scientific dig in Sweden. Her aunt was an archeologist, and she went on all sorts of adventures for her job. Meg wanted to be just like her when she grew up.

Meg wrapped her arms around her aunt's waist and squeezed tight. "You weren't supposed to be home until next week!" It had been two months since they'd last seen each other. Aunt Nikki's dreadlocks swooshed above Meg's head, and Meg breathed in her aunt's woodsy scent.

Uncle Derrick walked in and hugged Mom and Curtis while Aunt Nikki pulled Meg into the middle of the couch. Ruby and Tara settled down next to them.

"We found something amazing this time," Aunt Nikki said, "and we rushed home to study all the artifacts. Lucky for me, it also meant I could attend my favorite niece's birthday party."

Even though she had been waiting for the party to start, now that Aunt Nikki was here, Meg wanted to savor what was sure to be an incredible story. "Really? What did you find?" she asked.

Mom and Curtis sat across from them on the floor, a smile making Curtis's baby cheeks look even chubbier. Uncle Derrick stood behind them with his arms folded across his chest, impressed as always with his brilliant wife. Tara and Ruby leaned in closer to listen.

Aunt Nikki's voice deepened. "Our research took us to a little island off the coast of Sweden. There, we uncovered an ancient Viking burial ground where some believe their greatest warriors were put to rest."

Meg looked at her friends, sure that their astonished faces mirrored her own. She stared back at her aunt, whose gray eyes glowed. "On a hill above all the other graves sat a decorative tomb that clearly belonged to an important person. In it were the bones of what appeared to be a female Viking warrior."

"Whoa," Tara said. She looked from Meg to Aunt Nikki. "A *girl* warrior?"

"Yep," Aunt Nikki answered. "The very best kind."

Meg imagined what the warrior must have looked like with her armor and shield. She had almost forgotten where she was—in the middle of her own birthday party—when Mom interrupted her thoughts. "That's wonderful, Nikki, but I think it's time we celebrated this girl right here."

"Of course." Aunt Nikki stood and pulled Meg up next to her. She offered Ruby and Tara each a hand and pulled them up, too. "That's ancient history! Let's get back to the present where someone we all love is turning eight."

Chapter Three:
A Surprise Present

Everyone sat at the dining room table eating cake and ice cream. Curtis's face was so close to his bowl that a dot of peach frosting sat on his nose. Mom, Aunt Nikki, and Uncle Derrick all shared stories and laughed, catching up on the last two months while Meg and her friends took their empty bowls to the kitchen.

Noticing the girls had finished eating, Mom said, "What a fun party! But it's getting late and we should wrap things up."

"Or unwrap them!" Aunt Nikki said with a smile. "We can't forget the presents!"

They all moved to the living room and gathered around the coffee table, which was loaded with birthday presents. Meg knelt and opened Mom's package first, a bright new pair of orange sneakers with purple laces! She couldn't wait to zoom around the playground in them tomorrow.

Curtis gave her two new buttons to put on her backpack, one with a mustache and another with a llama that said "No Prob-llama." Meg had nearly covered half of her backpack already with her button collection.

Meg's dad sent her a beautiful shawl from Nigeria, where he was currently living. She couldn't wait to thank him during their next phone call!

Meg admired the illustrations in the book Ruby had given her. It was the latest in a mystery series by Meg's favorite author. Mom tried to hurry things along and told her she could thumb through the book later when she had more time.

Meg opened Tara's present, which was four bottles of bright nail polish. Her friend lined them up on the table, talking nonstop about their next sleepover and how they could paint and decorate one another's nails.

Meg picked her favorite color from the group. "I'm going to paint mine Bubblegum."

Ruby grabbed the bottle of sparkly green polish. "I'm painting mine Mermaid!"

"My favorite is Dragon," Tara said as she held out the shiny gold fingernail polish in her palm, oohing and aahing as if she were the star of a commercial.

Curtis snatched the last bottle of purple polish and held it high above his head. "Can I paint mine, too, Mama?"

The girls giggled, and Mom answered, "Maybe tomorrow, baby. Ruby and Tara's parents will be here soon to pick them up."

"But Meg hasn't opened our present yet."
Aunt Nikki reached into her pocket and set a
small box on the table in front of Meg.

Meg didn't even know that Aunt Nikki would be at her party. A present was an extra surprise. She studied the silver box, wanting to make this moment last as long as possible.

Tara clapped her hands. "Hurry up and open it."

Everyone watched anxiously.

"All right, all right," Meg said, slowly lifting the lid from the box. Inside, resting on a puffy bed of cotton, sat a thick silver ring with a scarlet stone. "It's . . . beautiful!" Meg whispered, hoping it would fit.

"We got it from a small market on the island," Aunt Nikki said.

Meg admired the fancy etchings on the silver band and slid it onto her middle finger, where it rested snuggly. A jolt shot from her finger to her arm and through her body, like an electric shock.

"Whoa," Meg said, feeling like something unusual had just happened.

Chapter Four:
Suddenly Sick

Aunt Nikki and Uncle Derrick stood up to leave. Meg went to give her aunt one last squeeze before they left, but she became dizzy and lost her balance. Ruby caught her by the arm and laughed. "I think someone had too much sugar."

Meg steadied herself and thanked everyone for coming. Mom's brow furrowed with worry. "Why don't you get ready for bed, sweetie? I'll make sure that everyone gets home okay."

Meg waved goodbye and weaved back to her room with Curtis on her heels. "Are you okay, Meg? You look a little woozy."

Her head throbbed, and her face felt flushed. "Can you please get me some water, C.? I'm thirsty."

While her brother ran to the kitchen, Meg changed into her pajamas and curled up in her bed. Curtis tumbled onto the covers next to her with a pink water bottle he had filled himself; she could hear the ice clinking inside.

"Are you going to be okay?" he asked, petting her long, spiral curls. Meg was feeling too sick to wrap her hair like she usually did.

"I'll be fine, Bubba." She called him by his baby nickname, and he let her because she felt sick.

Mom's swift footsteps sounded in the room, and soon her hand was pressed against Meg's forehead. "Hey, you have a fever," she said. "That came on pretty quickly."

With her eyes closed, it felt like Meg's bed had floated into the middle of the room where it spun around and around and around. Mom had her swallow some medicine and put a cool washrag on her forehead while Meg fought to keep her heavy eyelids from sinking.

Finally, Mom pulled Curtis from her bed, kissed Meg's forehead, and turned off the bedroom light.

Chapter Five:
Meg the Dream Warrior

Meg tossed and turned for a while before she finally settled down to sleep.

In her dream, she was on a lush island, standing at the edge of a cliff. A thick fog rolled in behind her as the sunset glowed pink on the horizon.

Meg's silver chain mail pulled at her
shoulders and the nose guard on her helmet
was distracting. But when she heard the
galloping of horses behind her, she knew
what she had to do.

Yelling out a war cry, she turned and ran directly toward the sound. Just as she saw the horses break through the fog, she leapt over the team, shooting to the sky like a powerful dragon.

She noticed every detail as she passed overhead, as if she were flying in slow motion. *Whoa*, Meg thought as she watched her legs scissor in the air. The soldiers on horseback looked up in amazement, a few reaching for their bows and arrows to try and ground her. Their leader cried out, and they struggled to turn the horses around.

Meg landed with a thud that shook her body. All her muscles flexed, and she felt strong. She ran ahead, dodging trees and bushes with animal-like reflexes. It was only then that she realized she carried a long sword in one hand and a shield in the other. She used them to block branches and brambles. The scenery zipped past her in a blur.

Horse hooves pounded behind her, but she pulled ahead and the sound faded. The woodland rose into a mountain, and Meg leapt up onto it, scaling it like a panther. When the ground finally became too steep for the horses, she heard their leader command the soldiers to retreat.

She slowed to a
jog and marched to
the mountain peak.
Her breathing was
even.

When she reached the top, she could see the entire island dropping beneath her like a ginormous ball gown. Meg marveled at how far she had come in just minutes, without even breaking a sweat. A grin stretched across her face and she couldn't help but throw her head back and laugh triumphantly.

She saw the twinkling of distant stars in the dusky sky, and her new ring flashed in the dying sunlight.

Chapter Six:
Super at School

When Meg woke up the next morning, she was sad to discover she had only been dreaming. Her heart still raced from the excitement of her imaginary adventure, and she sighed as she wondered how it would feel to be a *real* Viking warrior.

Meg held her hand among the rays of sunlight pouring through the window and smiled to see that her ring was still real. Aunt Nikki coming home in time for her birthday hadn't been part of her dream.

It took some convincing, but Mom finally relented and let Meg go to school after her sudden sickness the night before.

"But I feel fine now," Meg told Mom, talking through a mouthful of waffle. "And I want to show off my new sneakers." She held out her foot to demonstrate.

"Okay," Mom said. "But go to the nurse immediately if you start to feel sick again."

Meg and Curtis took off for school down the sidewalk, waving at Mom, who pulled out of the driveway in her car and drove in the opposite direction toward her office. Max, an old golden retriever that belonged to their neighbor, Dixie Wickerson, followed them to the stop sign, like he did every day.

Curtis buzzed the whole way about his favorite dinosaur, the *Allosaurus*. "Did you know that its name means 'different lizard,' because it looks like a lizard and it's so much bigger than the other dinosaurs? It's like, Godzilla big."

Meg nodded, feeling like they were walking bug-slow. She wanted to break into a run like she remembered from her dream the night before, but she knew she shouldn't get ahead of her little brother.

Before they separated at school, she reminded Curtis that Mom would pick him up from Homework Club, his two-day-a-week, after-school program. Meg liked Tuesdays and Thursdays because it gave her a break from having to walk her brother home from school so she could spend some time with Tara and Ruby.

Curtis called out to a couple friends and followed them toward his first-grade classroom. Meg turned down the third-grade hallway and into Ms. Clements's class.

The room hummed with chatter as she walked back to her seat. When she pulled the chair out from her desk, it slammed into the desk behind her. The room grew silent and everyone turned to stare at Meg. She shrank into the chair and waited quietly for the bell to ring.

After class started and everyone's attention was on Ms. Clements, Meg turned back to look at the desk behind her; there were two baseball-size dents where her chair had slammed into the metal.

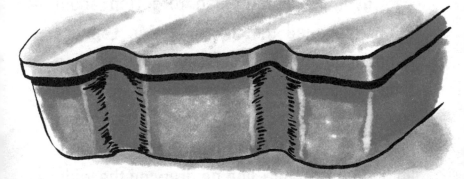

Did I do that? she wondered.

Chapter Seven:
The Disappearing Act

By gym class, Meg had forgotten about what happened that morning. Mr. Leonard announced that the class would be doing timed laps outside, and she was excited to run as fast as she could. He divided everyone into groups of five and had them take turns lining up on a chalk line he drew on the wide walking path that circled the playground.

The cool air nipped at Meg's fingertips, but she knew she would warm up as soon as she began to run. She stretched next to Tara, who was one of the fastest kids in class. "You're going to beat everyone with those cool shoes," her friend said, nodding at Meg's new, bright orange sneakers. They felt snug on her feet, and springy.

When Mr. Leonard called her group up, Meg stood on the outside of the track. Jackson, a tall boy from her class, stood next to her, crouching behind the line like an Olympic athlete waiting for the starting gun to go off.

"Good luck," Jackson said sarcastically to Meg and Tara. "You'll need it." Meg's stomach dropped, and she wondered when Jackson had grown so competitive.

Mr. Leonard counted down to the start of their run. When he shouted "go," Meg shot away from the line ahead of everyone else in her group. As in her dream, Meg didn't feel tired as she passed the climbing wall and swing sets. She wasn't even running as fast as she could. But when Meg realized she would cross the line before anyone else in her group was even halfway around the track, she knew something was different.

She slowed down and jogged to the finish line, still beating everyone else, but only by about ten feet.

"Wow! You moved like lightning!" Tara said, her mouth open in amazement. "How did you do that?"

Meg pretended to be out of breath so she wouldn't have to answer. But Tara's question still echoed in her mind. *How* did *I do that?* She snuck a peek at her ring, the scarlet stone blinking in the sunlight. It must have something to do with the Viking warrior ring.

Her super speed during gym was all Meg could think about for the rest of the day. She was so distracted by it that she didn't talk much to Ruby and Tara during lunch, and she gave them a silly excuse about having to go home right after school.

As she loaded up her backpack at her cubby outside Ms. Clements's class, Jackson called her name down the hallway. "It's Meg, the speed demon!" he yelled in a sneering voice. Meg's stomach twisted as Jackson neared, and she counted to ten, trying to calm her breathing as she waited for him to say something.

But when Jackson reached her, he looked all around, apparently unable to see Meg standing right there. His eyebrows bunched up, and then he shrugged and walked away. Meg turned to watch him go, and when she went to swing her backpack over her shoulder, she realized she couldn't see her own hands. Looking down at her body, Meg realized she couldn't see herself at all.

Meg had turned invisible!

Chapter Eight:
A Superpower Test

Meg went the back way home, cutting across the playground and through the big field that stretched across the empty blocks by her house. *What is happening?* she wondered as her mind spun from the craziness of the day. She ducked into a thicket of trees where she could be hidden while she tried to figure out what was going on.

In the grove, Meg could see birds perched in trees all the way across the field.

She closed her eyes and concentrated even harder. An argument between two brothers over a TV remote echoed in her ears. Meg's eyes snapped open to see where those boys might be, but she was too far away from any of the houses in her neighborhood to be able to hear something like that.

Meg told herself she needed to perform a few tests. She set her backpack down by the edge of the creek and jogged in place to warm up. Remembering her dream from the night before, when she leapt over the soldiers on horseback, Meg took a running jump over the creek.

She sprang high up in the air, easily clearing the treetops and flying toward the clouds. Her legs scissored beneath her and the air whooshed between her fingers as she started coming back down to the ground. Meg whooped when she landed and did a few more springy jumps toward the sky.

Remembering the two dents she had left in the desk at school earlier, Meg jumped into the middle of the creek and, pushing her shoulder against a boulder in the rushing water, she rolled it up one side of the creek until both she and the giant stone rested in the dry dirt. Laughing at the energy zinging through her body, Meg sped around the field as fast as she could, her body disappearing into a blur.

When she finally started to get tired, Meg took off her ring and dropped it into the outside pocket of her backpack. She had to know if it was the ring giving her these powers. Taking a running start, Meg leapt as high as she could, lifting only two feet from the ground before crashing into the dirt.

Her knee hurt, and her eyes stung from the pain. She grabbed a fallen leaf and used it to brush all the mud and gravel away from the scrape.

Meg pulled Aunt Nikki's present from the pocket of her backpack and slipped it over her finger again. She ran through all the things that had happened that day, holding up fingers as she counted:

Invisibility.

Super-senses.

Super-strength.

Super-speed.

A sharp tingle traveled down her back as Meg realized that her birthday ring had given her... superpowers!

Chapter Nine:
Choosing to Be Brave

Walking home through the field, Meg thought about what she should do with her newfound powers. She was too young to fight crime, and she was pretty sure Mom wouldn't approve of it anyway. Plus, Meg was a little shy sometimes, and she liked to keep to herself. Becoming a superhero might result in receiving a little more attention than she was comfortable with.

Meg kicked her way through the high grass as she realized that until she knew what she was going to do with these powers, she should keep everything secret. She shouldn't tell Mom and Curtis, or Tara and Ruby.

As she continued to think about her amazing discovery, a bubbling sound began to pound at her ears. *Someone must be boiling water for macaroni and cheese*, Meg thought. Super-hearing might get distracting after a while.

She went back to thinking about her powers. If a friend had a beautiful voice, wouldn't Meg encourage her to sing? Especially if her friend's singing could help other people be happier? Maybe part of having superpowers meant that Meg would have to use them to help people. She wasn't sure she was brave enough to do that.

The bubbling sound became so loud, Meg stopped walking to look around.

The small stream she had been following had gotten wider. She looked behind her to see that the gushing was coming from the middle of the creek, where the water gurgled like a geyser. It came from the same spot the boulder had been before she moved it.

The creek was now flooding over its banks, soaking Meg's new sneakers in the process.

This could be bad, she thought and backed away from the water. The stream suddenly became a narrow river with rough waves pulling bushes and sticks into its current. Backing up some more, Meg worried about her neighborhood. Would her house be swept away in a flood?

79

A dog's whimper turned Meg's attention forward. She saw that the water had pulled in old Max, her neighbor's dog, and he was being carried downstream. She had to help him! But her heart hammered in her chest, and her stomach twisted. She looked at her hands to discover that her fear had turned her invisible. Maybe Meg wasn't cut out to be a superhero after all.

Max's barking stopped and his head dipped beneath the water. *Max needed help now!*

Meg dropped her backpack from her shoulders and jumped to the bank closest to where Max had been pulled under. *Can I super-swim, too?* she wondered.

A few feet ahead, the base of a small tree dipped beneath the water line. Meg ran over to the tree and pushed against it until the trunk snapped, causing it to fall. Now the broken tree crossed the raging water like a bridge, and Meg carefully walked to where Max was struggling.

She scooped him from the water and leapt from her makeshift bridge. The force of her jump broke the tree in half, and its pieces were carried away. She laid Max on dry ground until he caught his breath and slowly stood. While he recovered, Meg jumped back to where she had moved the boulder earlier and rolled it back to the middle of the creek, plugging the geyser.

The gurgling sound of the water stopped, and within seconds, the river shrank back to its normal size.

As Meg tried to dry Max off with a jacket she pulled from her backpack, Max licked her cheeks in thanks.

Chapter Ten:
Home in Time for Dinner

Meg and Max walked home slowly as the dog recovered from his scare. She led him across the street to Dixie's house and made sure to shut him inside the gate. She was done saving dogs for the night.

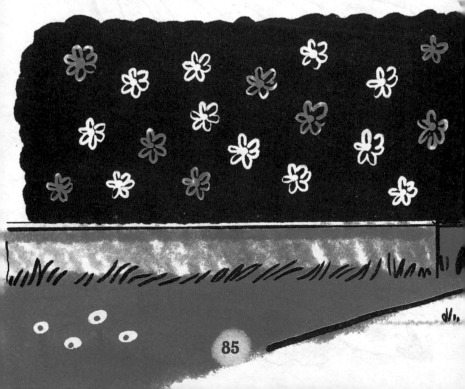

Crossing the street and heading toward her house, she thought the branches of their maple tree were glowing in the dusk. She shook her head, certain she was seeing things, but then the leaves flew away. Meg realized they weren't leaves at all, but hundreds of glowing moths.

Her superpowers weren't the only strange thing that had happened that day.

Meg thought back to the gurgling creek overflowing in the field. And now the tree full of glowing moths. What was happening in her ordinary town of Plainview?

Meg opened the door to her house and kicked her soggy sneakers off in the entryway. Curtis sat at the dining room table doing his homework, and she could hear Mom bustling in the kitchen.

"Is that you, Meg?" she called.

"Yes," Meg answered back, breathing in the scent of her favorite dinner—spaghetti with meatballs.

"It's starting to get dark out there!" Mom said, walking from the kitchen. She wiped her hands on a towel draped over one shoulder. She looked frustrated. "Next time, please tell me when you're staying late at Ruby's house so I can give you a ride home."

A knot formed in Meg's chest as she realized that keeping her secret from Mom meant she'd have to lie sometimes. "I'm sorry," Meg said, and the apology was more for her dishonesty than it was for being late.

"Are you hungry?" she asked.

"I'm starving!" Meg said, and *that* was the truth.

"Help your brother finish his homework first," Mom said. "And then we'll eat."

Meg peeked over Curtis's shoulder as he worked on a vocabulary worksheet. He only had one more sentence to fill in before he was done. "Although she was small, she was strong and _ _ _ _ _ _."

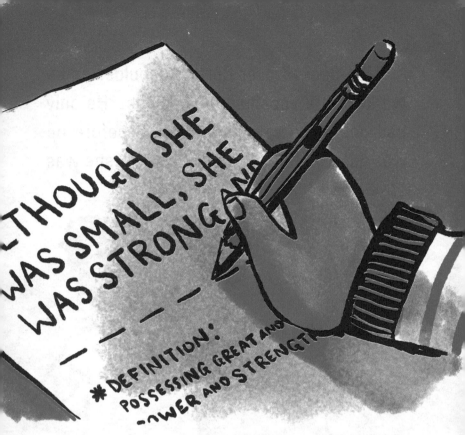

THOUGH SHE
WAS SMALL, SHE
WAS STRONG

* DEFINITION:
POSSESSING GREAT AND
POWER AND STRENGTH

"There's only one word left." Meg tried giving him a clue instead of telling him the answer. She read the word's definition to herself: *possessing great and impressive power and strength.*

"Uh . . . mighty?" Curtis asked.

"Mighty!" Meg confirmed.

94

She realized that even though she was scared at first, she had still saved Max from drowning earlier, which was exactly the kind of thing a superhero would do. Maybe Meg could be brave enough to help people who needed it. Smiling to herself, Meg imagined wearing a fancy costume with a cape and double Ms on her chest, because she already knew what her superhero name would be. Mighty Meg.

Read on for a sneak peek from the second book in the **Mighty Meg** series.

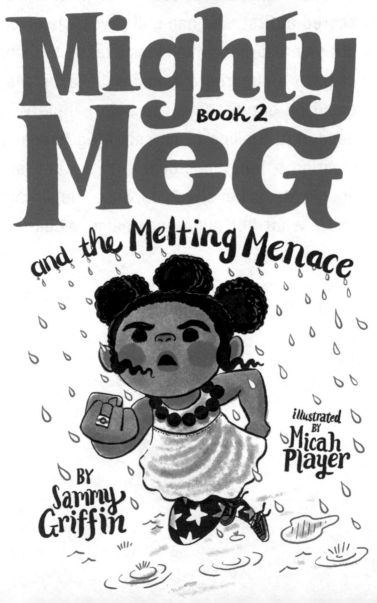

Mighty Meg

BOOK 2

and the Melting Menace

illustrated BY Micah Player

BY Sammy Griffin

Chapter One:
In the Hot Seat at Dinner

Meg snuck in through the side door of her house. She hung her jacket on a hook and kicked her shoes off in the mudroom.

"Meg?" Mom called from the kitchen.

She had hoped to make it to her room before anyone realized she was home. "Hi, Mom!" Meg walked over to where her mom stood by the stove, flipping grilled cheeses.

"How was school today, honey?" Mom looked tired. Her feet were bare, but she still wore her grey business jacket and skirt.

Meg leaned in for a half hug as Mom used the spatula in her free hand to flip grilled cheese sandwiches. "Good."

"What have you and the girls been up to?" Mom asked. "You haven't said much about Ruby and Tara lately."

This past week, Meg had been testing her new superpowers after school. She practiced in the open field by her house, using her super-speed to run around the field, her super-strength to lift heavy rocks, and her heightened senses to see and hear faraway animals. She was even working on controlling her invisibility, so she would stop turning invisible whenever she was scared. Meg hadn't been to either of her friends' houses to do homework with them like usual, but Mom didn't know that.

Meg shrugged. "Um . . . not much."

"Why don't you and Curtis set the table, and we'll talk more about your day over dinner."

Meg groaned to herself. She would have to figure out a way to get her brother to do all the talking. *Dinosaurs!* She smiled. If she asked Curtis about *Velociraptors*, he would talk all night.

"Curtis!" Meg called her brother away from the TV in the living room. He reluctantly stood and came into the kitchen to help, the sound from his nature program still blaring in the background.

As Meg handed him the plates, he asked, "Did you know some scientists want to create a *Chickenosaurus*?" Curtis spent the next ten minutes talking about how cool a chicken dinosaur would be. By the time he had turned off the television and sat down to eat, he was dinosaured out.

Mom ladled soup into their bowls and passed around the plate of grilled cheese sandwiches. Before anyone had even taken a bite, Curtis turned all the attention back to Meg as he said, "On my way to Homework Club today, I saw Tara and Ruby leave school without Meg." He slurped up a spoonful of soup, leaving a thick red mustache on his lip.

"Manners." Mom pushed Curtis's napkin toward him before turning to Meg. "Where were you, sweetie?"

Meg's cheeks flushed as she thought back to an afternoon spent jumping up into the tallest branches of the oak tree in the field by their house. It may sound like an easy feat for someone with superpowers, but apparently her super-jumping abilities did not come with super-coordination.

Meg had been practicing jumping all week, but it still took her quite a few tries to stick the landings.

"Looking for a book at the library," Meg lied, staring at her soup as if it were the most interesting thing she'd ever seen.

"Oh, really?" Mom swallowed a spoonful of soup before asking, "What book?"

"I didn't actually find it." Meg pulled at the crust on her sandwich. "It's a new book in a series, and the school doesn't have it yet."

"Ah, that's too bad," Mom said, and then she asked Curtis what he was reading in school these days.

Meg relaxed back into her seat, happy to have all the attention diverted away from her. But then she realized how easily Mom had believed her lie, and she felt even worse.

Sammy Griffin is a children's book author and super-geek who fangirls over superheroes and comic books in real life. She lives in Idaho Falls, Idaho, with her super-geek family.

Micah Player was born in Alaska and now lives in the mountains of Utah with a schoolteacher named Stephanie. They are the parents of two rad kids, one brash Yorkshire terrier, and several Casio keyboards.

micahplayer.com

Journey to some magical places and outer space, rock out, and soar among the clouds with these other chapter book series from Little Bee Books!

Tales of **SASHA** #1
The Big Secret
by Alexa Pearl
Illustrated by Paco Sordo

ELLA AND **OWEN** BOOK 1
THE CAVE OF AAAAAH! DOOM!
by Jaden Kent
Illustrated by Iryna Bodnaruk

THE **ALIEN** NEXT DOOR
THE NEW KID
BY A. I. NEWTON   ILLUSTRATED BY ANJAN SARKAR

little bee books
an imprint of Bonnier Publishing USA